RIGHTY and LEFTY
A Tale of Two Feet

By RACHEL VAIL

Illustrations by MATTHEW CORDELL

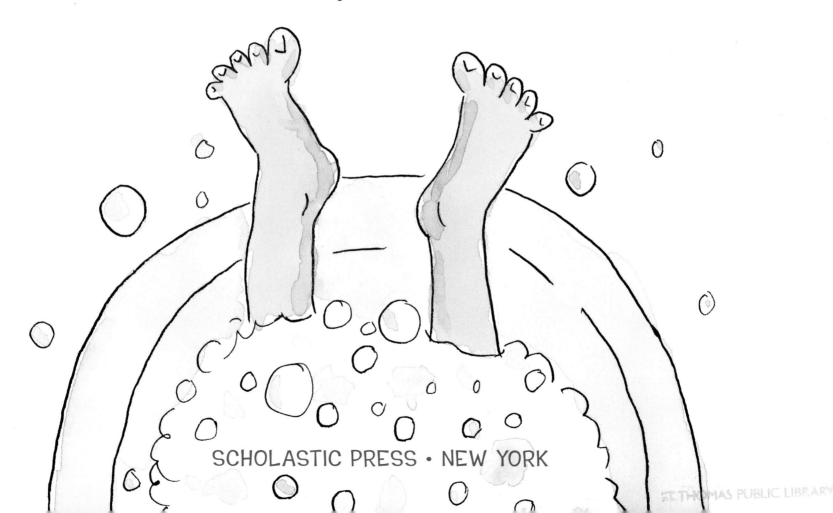

SCHOLASTIC PRESS • NEW YORK

Library of Congress Cataloging-in-Publication Data

Vail, Rachel.
Righty & Lefty / by Rachel Vail ; illustrated by Matthew Cordell. — 1st ed.   p. cm.
Summary: Even though Lefty and Righty like different things, they find they must learn to get along together without tripping over each other.
[1. Foot—Fiction. 2. Cooperativeness—Fiction. 3. Friendship—Fiction.]
I. Cordell, Matthew, 1975– ill. II. Title. III. Title: Righty and Lefty. PZ7.V1916Le 2007   [E]—dc22   2006028840
ISBN 13: 978-0-439-63629-2   ISBN 10: 0-439-63629-9

10 9 8 7 6 5 4 3 2 1   07 08 09 10 11

Printed in Singapore
First edition, November 2007

The text type was set in Coop Light. The display type was set in Coop Heavy. The illustrations were done in pen and ink and watercolor.

Book design by Lillie Mear

For Liam and Zachary

– R.V.

To Julie, for loving me and

shoes eternally

– M.C.

This is Righty.

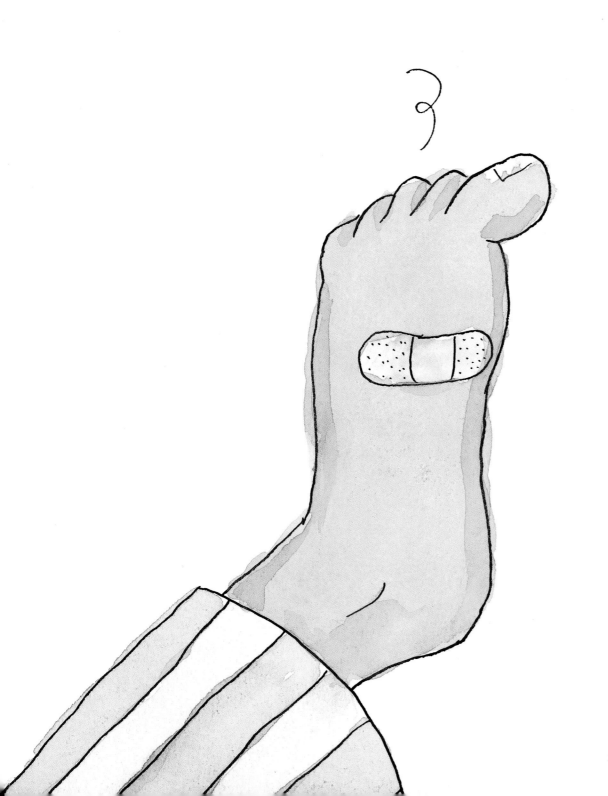

This is Lefty.

Righty and Lefty don't always get along so well,
but they are stuck with each other because
they are two feet on one person.

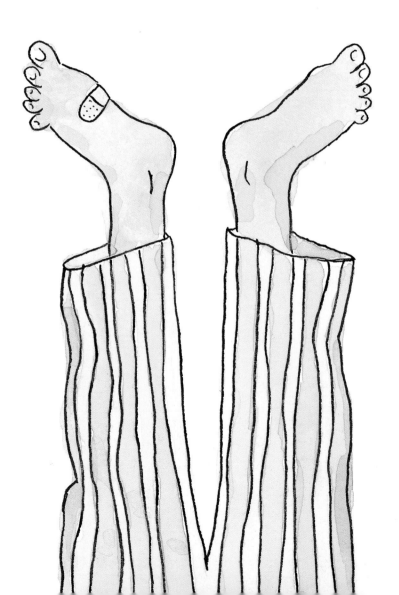

Righty is ready to go places.

Lefty is a little cold and would like a few more

minutes under the blankets.

Lefty's sock has a hole.

Righty says, "Don't worry. It's a very small hole."

"I'm practically naked," groans Lefty.

Righty likes every shoe.

Lefty only likes galoshes.
"Galoshes?" asks Righty.
"Galoshes?!"

"Galoshes are puddle-proof," says Lefty.
"Good point," Righty agrees.

If they work together, they can do tricks.
This is their best trick.

Until Lefty gets distracted,
and Righty gets clobbered.

and hides.

up,

up,

up,

Righty goes away,

Lefty is sorry for getting distracted.
Lefty taps a bit, waiting, waiting,
lonely down alone on the linoleum.
It is no fun to be Lefty without Righty.

When Righty comes back down,
Lefty wants to play.
But Righty has fallen asleep,
and needs to be stomped.

Outside, Righty and Lefty race.
Sometimes, Righty wins.

Sometimes, Lefty wins.

It is always close.

If Righty wins, Lefty is a sore loser.

But not for very long.

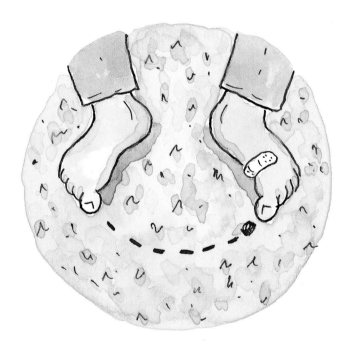

Righty kicks a rock to Lefty.

Lefty kicks it back.

It is their favorite game.

Righty loves to look at grown-up shoes. There are so many possible options.

Lefty is unconvinced.

"I'm never wearing shoes," grumbles Lefty.

"When I grow up, I'm wearing galoshes every day."

"You only get one," says Righty. "You will have to wear a galosh."

Sometimes Righty imagines taking a
beach vacation without Lefty.

They help each other out of their sneakers.

"Ew," says Lefty. "You stink."

"You stink, too," says Righty.

"I know," says Lefty. "We are quite a pair."

They chase each other around.

It's always fun until someone gets hurt.

A boo-boo bunny comes to help.
It has no legs and is freezing cold.
Lefty does not trust this bunny.

Lefty does not like the nail clippers, either.

Or being tickled.
(Well, maybe a little,
but not much.)

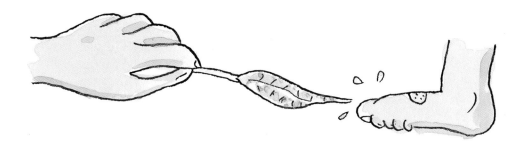

Or the bath.

"Just relax and enjoy it," says Righty, under the towel.

"Oh," moans Lefty. "Life is a blister."

Righty doesn't want to go to bed yet. Righty thinks it's not fair that just because Lefty is tired and cranky, they should both have to go to bed. Righty hangs down the side, swinging.

It's dark. There's nothing to do.
Righty's slipper falls off.
It is no fun to be Righty without Lefty.

Righty slides under the covers.

Lefty is cozy and warm.

Righty snuggles up beside Lefty.

"Good night, Lefty," says Righty.

"Mmm," says Lefty dreamily.

"Galoshes."